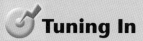
Tuning In

Caring for Our World can be read from b[eginning to end. It] may also be read by choosing a section [to focus on.] The teaching notes take this into accou[nt, however, pages 2-] 3 are an introduction and should be read first.

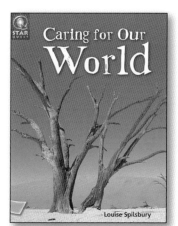

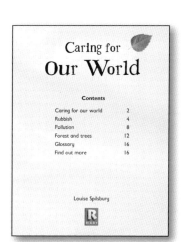

The front cover

Read the title.

Speaking and Listening

Why do we need to care for our world?

What could be some of the headings in the list of contents?

The back cover

Read the blurb to find out more.

Contents

Read through the list of contents.
What does 'pollution' mean?
Where can we look to check the meaning?

Speaking and Listening

Can you think of a question beginning with 'Where' or 'How' to ask about rubbish?

Can you think of a question beginning with 'What', 'Where' or 'How' to ask about pollution?

Can you think of a question beginning with 'How' or 'Why' to ask about forests?

As we read each section we are going to see if we can find the answers.

READ

Read pages 2 and 3

Purpose: to find out why it is important to care for our world.

PAUSE

Pause at page 3

What does 'environment' mean? Where can you look to find out?

Speaking and Listening

Why do you think the children have decided to find out how they can help care for our world?

Caring for our world

I saw a television programme about the **environment**. It made me think about what I can do to look after our world. I told my friends at school about the environment. We decided to find out how we can help.

We found out about **pollution**.

We found out about trees and forests.

We found out about all the rubbish in the world.

Read pages 4 and 5

Purpose: to find out how rubbish is a problem.

Pause at page 5

What were the questions you thought of for rubbish?

Have the questions been answered in the text?

Which words would you expect to find in the glossary?

Speaking and Listening

Where would you go to find your local council?

Rubbish

Did you know that every year, we throw away more than 434 million tonnes of rubbish in the UK? Our rubbish comes from factories, offices, shops and houses. 1 tonne of rubbish is thrown away from every house in the UK each year – that's a total of 27 million tonnes of rubbish! We wondered where it all goes.

We went to see someone at our **local council** to find out.

There are lots of places where rubbish can be recycled – but it needs organising first.

A lot of waste goes to **landfill sites**. However, landfill sites are ugly and take up valuable land that could be a park or an open space.

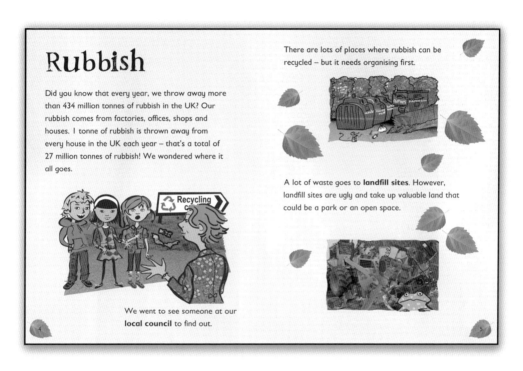

READ

Read pages 6 and 7

Purpose: to find what we can do to help solve the problem of rubbish.

PAUSE

Pause at page 7

What were three things they did to help solve the problem of rubbish?

Speaking and Listening

Look up 'campaign' in the glossary.

How would you start a campaign in our school to tidy up the playground?

What we did about rubbish

We decided that we could:
- recycle more
- re-use more
- pick up litter.

We started rinsing and sorting bottles before putting them into bottle banks.

We stopped throwing away unwanted clothes, toys and books. Instead, we took them to a charity shop where they can be sold to help others.

At school, we started a **campaign** to tidy up the playing fields.

Read pages 8 and 9

Purpose: to find out what causes pollution.

Pause at page 9

What is the main thing that pollutes the air?

Check the glossary to find out what 'carbon dioxide' is.

Speaking and Listening

What would a polluted river look like?

What could be some of the ways we could help reduce pollution?

Pollution

We found out that pollution is waste that has got into the environment. It comes from our factories, cars and lorries. It also comes from ships that spill oil into our seas and oceans.

We went to see a polluted river. We learnt that pollution can kill the plants and animals that live there.

Oil spills at sea can cause a lot of harm to sea life.

The air is made unhealthy by **carbon dioxide** from car exhausts, factories and power stations. In the UK, about 152 million tonnes of carbon dioxide are pumped into the air each year.

Read pages 10 and 11

Purpose: to find out what the children did to help reduce pollution.

Pause at page 11

What questions did you think of for pollution?

Have you found the answers in the text?

Speaking and Listening

The children thought of three ways they could help reduce pollution. Are they the same ones you thought of?

What things can our class do to help reduce pollution?

What we did about pollution

There is a lot we can do to help reduce pollution:

- walk or cycle to school
- take the bus or train instead of the car
- use **environmentally friendly** cleaning products.

We started walking and cycling to school.

We used soaps, washing powders and cleaning liquids that don't harm the environment.

We tried to travel by bus or train instead of by car. One bus or train can carry the same amount of people as a lot of cars, but causes less pollution.

Read pages 12 and 13

Purpose: to find out why it is important to look after the rainforests.

Pause at page 13

What were the questions you thought of for forests?

Have the questions been answered in the text?

Speaking and Listening

What do you think the children will think of to help protect the rainforests?

Forests and trees

Did you know that every two seconds an area of forest the size of a football pitch is destroyed? Our **rainforests** provide a home for most of the animals that live on land. They also keep our air healthy by absorbing harmful gases like carbon dioxide.

We learnt that if we don't protect our rainforests, in 50 years every rainforest on Earth will be gone.

Rainforests are burnt to clear land to mine for oil and minerals, and to keep cattle on. They are also cut down for **timber**, cardboard and paper.

If we keep cutting down our rainforests the animals that live there will disappear.

Read pages 14 and 15

Purpose: to find out what we can do to help protect the rainforests.

Pause at page 15

What does 'sponsor' the rainforest mean?

What does 'recycle' mean?

Speaking and Listening

What can we do in this class to help save the rainforests?

What we did to save our forests

We decided that to protect our trees we would:

- **sponsor** the rainforests
- recycle paper
- plant trees.

We recycled all of our paper, and used both sides to write or draw on.

We planted trees. Our trees will make a home for wildlife and help to keep our air healthy.

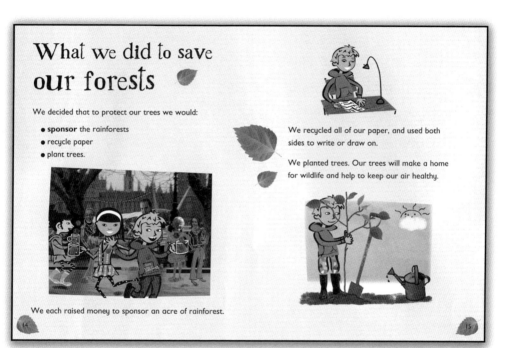

We each raised money to sponsor an acre of rainforest.

Read page 16

Purpose: to check we can read all the scientific words in the text.

Pause at page 16

Let's read all the words in bold together.

Speaking and Listening

In which part of the text did we read about:

carbon dioxide?

landfill sites?

campaign?